D0250556

ROSCO THE RASCAL
VISITS THE
PUMPKIN PATCH

Rosco the Rascal #1

By Shana Gorian

Illustrated by Ros Webb

Cover art by Josh Addessi

Rosco The Rascal Visits The Pumpkin Patch.
Copyright © 2014 by Shana Gorian. All Rights Reserved.

Illustrations by Ros Webb.
Cover design by Kim Killion.
Cover art by Josh Addessi.

All rights reserved under International and Pan American
Copyright conventions. No part of this book may be
reproduced, transmitted, downloaded, recorded, or stored in
any information storage and retrieval system, in any form or
by any means, whether electronic or mechanical, now known
or hereinafter invented, without the express written
permission of the publisher, except for brief quotations for
review purposes.

This is a work of fiction. Names, characters, places, and
incidents are products of the author's imagination or are
used fictitiously and are not to be construed as real. Any
resemblance to actual events, locales, organizations, or
persons, living or dead, is entirely coincidental.

First Edition, 2014

*Knowing what's right
doesn't mean much unless you
do what's right.*

~Theodore Roosevelt

CONTENTS

CHAPTER 1

KEEP-AWAY

It was a beautiful September morning. Ten-year-old James and seven-year-old Mandy McKendrick thought they couldn't sit still one minute longer. It had been a long drive.

"We're here—finally," James announced.

The minivan came to a stop in the farm's parking lot. James pushed the button to open the automatic sliding door next to his seat.

The door slid open, and Rosco, their German shepherd, leaped out before anyone could stop him.

"Rosco, come back here! Bad dog!" called Mandy. But her shouts were useless. A small pumpkin was on the move, and it had caught

Rosco's eye as they'd approached the farm.

Rosco had never seen a pumpkin before. As it rolled down a gentle hill, he thought it looked like something he'd love to chase.

It was early in the morning, and not many people had arrived on the farm yet. The wide, grassy field was empty except for this lively dog.

A man wearing a western hat reached out to stop the rest of his pumpkins from rolling out of the wheelbarrow as Rosco raced after the pumpkin.

Brother and sister James and Mandy jumped out of the minivan, exchanging a worried look. This kind of thing had never happened on their trip to the pumpkin patch before. Their rascally, large dog was already at least fifty feet away from them and still running at breakneck speed.

"Uh oh," Mandy said slowly. She watched as Rosco caught up to the pumpkin and sank his big teeth straight into the stem.

Then Rosco lifted his head. The pumpkin

had become stuck in his teeth!

"Oh, my goodness!" Mom said as she approached.

But Rosco didn't mind the pumpkin being stuck there and began to run again. He ran toward the man in the hat, coming just close enough to tease him. The man tried to grab the pumpkin from him. But Rosco stayed out of reach. *I love to play keep-away,*

Rosco thought.

Even with a pumpkin stuck in his teeth, Rosco still wore a mischievous grin.

"Come here, pooch!" the man called, smiling.

The kids now stood near the man, trying to coax Rosco back. Their mom and dad started to cross the field toward them, hollering this and that. But nothing worked.

"Rosco, come here! That's not yours! Give it back!" ordered Mandy. "You'll get your own pumpkin later!"

James started to chase Rosco, but that made Rosco run even faster because he wanted to be chased. The dog switched directions every time James got close. His tail wagged every time he slowed down. *This game never gets old,* Rosco thought.

"He's only going to keep running away if you chase him," Mandy said.

Rosco ran another wide circle around them, and then trotted closer. Mandy started for his collar, but he bolted away before she could reach him.

Who wants to try next? Rosco thought.

But Mandy had run out of patience. Everyone else had too, except for Rosco. Mandy stomped her foot. "Give it to me, Rosco! Now!"

The man in the hat had another idea. "Here, boy." He held out one hand to the dog.

"I won't chase you, buddy," he explained softly. "My kids are over there waiting, and I know you're too fast for me."

He turned and waved to three small children and a sweet looking woman next to a silver pick-up truck. They waved back.

He pointed to the pumpkin in Rosco's mouth. "My son picked that one out all by himself this morning. He was really hoping to carve it into a jack-o-lantern come late October. And we have to be on our way soon."

Rosco listened, tilting his head to one side. He trotted up to the man, sat down, and lowered his head. The doggy smile finally disappeared. His eyes now bore an apology.

Rosco tried to let the pumpkin go, but it was still stuck. He was beginning to drool all over it.

Rosco wanted this nice man's son to have his pumpkin back. He didn't want to spoil anyone's fun. He had only wanted to have a little fun of his own.

The man squatted down in front of the dog. He reached out kindly and pulled the pumpkin from Rosco's teeth, quite surprised to have it returned. Rosco's fangs had done some damage. Two deep holes were left. But the pumpkin was still in one piece.

"Well, there we are! I guess we can still carve this, you ol' rascal," the man decided. "What's your dog's name?" he said to the kids.

James told him that his rascal of a dog was named Rosco.

"Well, Rosco, I thought this pumpkin was a 'goner! But I think it'll be fine..."

He picked up the small pumpkin and waved it at his kids. They cheered for their dad and the big, shiny, black dog that had put on such an entertaining show.

Mandy apologized for her dog and told the man that Rosco was still just a big puppy. "He can be incorrigible at times, or so my mother says."

"No harm done," said the man.

He gave Rosco a tough look, then grinned widely at him, nodding to Mandy, James, and Mr. and Mrs. McKendrick.

Mandy reached for Rosco's leash from Mom and fastened it onto his collar.

"Leave other people's pumpkins alone next time," Mandy warned Rosco. Then she scratched his soft head as she whispered to him, "But you're a good boy for giving it back!"

CHAPTER 2

NEW MEMBER OF THE FAMILY

James and Mandy McKendrick visited the pumpkin patch every fall with their mother and father. It had become a late September tradition for them. They loved the cool and foggy mornings on the drive over, and the warm, sunny days at the farm.

The drive took about an hour, and the McKendrick family always arrived as soon as the farm opened its gates.

They wanted to beat the Saturday morning rush. People came from miles around to taste a bit of the country life each fall.

They'd marvel at the red and orange

leaves on the trees. They'd gaze at the wide-open fields, and inhale the fresh, country smell of barn and field.

"But line up for that pony ride by 9:00 a.m. sharp or you'll wait for an hour!" their dad always said.

So, the family carefully planned their day. First came the pony ride.

"I want the white one!" Mandy said when she was younger. She knew she *should* want a brown one, to match her long brown hair, but she didn't. She always wanted a white one.

"I just can't help it," she'd say. This year Mom had asked if the color of the pony was going to matter today, now that she was a whole year older, and she had replied "No." Then, she said, "Well, maybe..."

James, with his red hair and freckles, was not so choosy. He had always been happy with any sort of pony when he was younger, but he told them on the drive over that he was getting too old for ponies.

"I'm ten now. I went horseback riding

this summer. This is way too easy," he said.

It was true. It *was* easy. Each of the ponies was tied to the one in front of it, and they only went around in a big circle. So James had announced that he would just sit and wait while Mandy rode this year.

"You sure?" his dad asked.

"Yep."

"Well, I still want to ride one even if James doesn't!" Mandy said.

After a tasty lunch, the corn maze, and maybe a hayride, they'd always end their day by picking out pumpkins.

But this year's visit was going to be different, not just because the kids were getting older. It was because the McKendricks had made a charming new addition to the family last summer, and they had brought him along today.

He stood on four legs and they named him Rosco. He was a German shepherd, almost fully-grown. He weighed eighty-five pounds and was turning two years old this month.

His color was mostly black. He had friendly, dark eyes, tan legs, and a little bit of white fur on his paws and face.

"He's so adorable!" Mandy said, when Dad first brought him home.

"Awesome!" were the only words that came from James's mouth, but the look on his face said that he completely agreed with

Mandy.

Rosco was playful and full of energy, and always seemed to be wearing a friendly doggy grin.

James especially loved having someone around who was always ready to play, no matter what the game: fetch, chase, tug of war, or race-ya!

Also, James liked to hang out with the dog because he and Rosco never got into fights with each other. Like many brothers and sisters, James and Mandy argued every so often.

But Rosco was always easy to get along with. Mandy had taught Rosco to jump over the picnic table bench in their yard, shake hands with his paw, and catch a tennis ball right out of the air.

Mandy also liked having someone who liked quiet time as much as she did. Sometimes she would lay her head over the back of Rosco's neck when he was sprawled out on the floor and use him as a pillow.

Rosco had a terribly loud and frightening bark. His bark scared off the coyotes that sometimes roamed the hills surrounding their house, so Mandy and James always felt safe with Rosco around.

Rosco had become such a favorite of the McKendricks that he now went nearly everywhere they did, or at least as often as Mom would allow.

"He does seem to find trouble easily enough," Mom would say when she was trying to be agreeable and not give them an outright "No".

"Yes, but he doesn't mean to," Mandy would say.

More often than not these days, the kids got their way, and Rosco came along to wherever it was that the family was going.

So Rosco's tail wagged quickly as the family walked toward the pony ride this beautiful Saturday morning.

Rosco was happy that he'd only been put on a leash and not been punished after the pumpkin incident. *Lucky break. Next time, I'd better think first and stay out of trouble,* he thought.

CHAPTER 3

THE LEASH

Crowds were arriving at the farm. Rosco walked beside his people. James held the leash.

They were on their way to the pony ride.

"We'll hit the petting zoo next, Dad, right?" Mandy asked.

"That's right, Sweetie."

Rosco silently promised them that he would be on his best behavior for the rest of the day.

A moment later, however, a funny noise caught his attention. Rosco's ears perked up. Was it a rooster? No, he had heard what the kids called a rooster earlier, and this was different.

Rosco stopped for a moment to listen. He pulled on the leash with his neck just slightly, so he could stay where he was and keep listening. James tugged back.

"Come on, Rosco," James said. "We need to get in line."

Rosco followed. *I have no choice with this leash on,* he thought. He tugged at it again, trying hard to listen for the source of the funny noise.

"Your father and I are going to buy Mandy a ticket over there," Mom called, pointing at the ticket booth. "You kids stay in line." A small crowd of children and parents began to form between them.

"Here, take Rosco!" James shouted over the crowd. "He doesn't want to stand still."

James dropped the leash to let Rosco walk to Mom. Rosco slipped through the crowd and headed straight for her. But Mom hadn't heard James at all, and didn't notice Rosco coming towards her.

Mandy pointed to the ponies. "Look,

James! There's a white one this year!"

"Oh, cool," said James, turning to look.

Just then Rosco heard the funny noise again. No one noticed as he trotted off to investigate, his leash dragging behind him. *I'll only be gone a minute. They won't even notice.*

CHAPTER 4

ROSCO AND
THE GOOSE

Soon Rosco's ears brought him to a pen full of more funny noises. He stood on his hind legs to get a better view over the fence. Ducks large and small waddled about. Rabbits hopped. Baby goats allowed eager kids to feed them and pet their soft backs. Little pigs raced about.

A petting zoo! This must be what the kids were talking about in the car. Baby animals. He gazed intently over the fence.

In the next moment he found himself
face to face with a very tall, white goose with
a long, orange beak, and she wasn't smiling.
The goose honked loudly at him. *Yes, this
was the sound!*

Rosco barked once at the goose. The
goose honked. Rosco barked again. The goose
honked some more. *This gal wants to play!*

The goose waddled about, now angry at
the barking dog. She didn't want to play at all.
I hope she knows I'm only playing around,
Rosco thought. He kept barking. His leash

dangled from his neck, dragging across the ground.

A moment later, the angry goose waddled backward, honking at Rosco and waving her head back and forth. But she wasn't watching where she was going and backed up into a little girl!

The little girl toppled over. As she gazed in fear at the sharp beak pointed at her, the girl jumped to her feet and ran for the gate. Yanking it open, she screamed with all her might. "Daddy!"

The little girl ran out of the gate and in a moment, her father scooped her up, safe and sound.

But the damage had been done. The gate was left open. Five baby sheep quickly trotted out of the pen and into the open grass! Off they ran, scattering into the open field nearby.

Ah-oh, Rosco thought.

Rosco set to work. He had shepherd in his blood, and this was his chance to shine.

He raced up behind the sheep.

This made the sheep flock together for safety. Then, he kept running behind, so they'd move in the direction that he wanted them to move. Soon, they headed back toward the pen. Rosco's leash trailed behind him as he followed.

In no time at all, the sheep crowded back into the corral with Rosco close behind.

"Close the gate!" hollered a farmhand to the attendant. Rosco sat down outside the pen, panting away.

The farmhand walked up. He stooped

down and grabbed Rosco's leash to look at the tags on his collar. "Rosco, is it? Why, you old rascal, Rosco. You should've known better than to bother my nasty old goose! But at least you brought my sheep back. Thanks, pal!"

He gave him a hearty pat on the back. Several kids had gathered around now to pet the hero dog.

Rosco wagged his tail, gave the farmhand his warm, doggy grin, and trotted off. *You're welcome, sir!*

By this time Mandy had taken her turn on the pony. Mom, Dad, and James had watched her from the other side of the fence. Mandy walked over to the three of them. Right then, Rosco skipped up. His leash was still dragging on the ground and had become rather dirty. He wagged his tail and panted.

James poured some water into the collapsible bowl they used for outings with the dog. Rosco drank rapidly.

Mom turned to the dog. "Well, where

have *you* been, Rosco?" She patted his back.

"James, did you let him walk around by himself and forget to take off his leash?"

James looked confused.

"What? I sent him over to you. Remember? Before the pony ride."

Mom looked at James.

"I have no idea what you're talking about," she said.

Then everyone looked at Rosco, wondering what he had been up to now.

"Where did you go, Rosco?" Dad said, not expecting an answer from a dog.

"I guess we'll never know," Mom said. She lowered her eyebrows, questioning.

No answer came, of course. Rosco drooled and smiled. Water dripped from his tongue.

Mandy ran ahead. "Let's go see the petting zoo!"

CHAPTER 5

THE HAYRIDE

"Let's give Rosco a second chance, Mom. Can I take off his leash now?" Mandy said.

"Well, sure, honey, he seems tired out anyway. He'll probably stay out of trouble for a while," said Mom. Mandy unfastened the leash and handed it to Mom.

Rosco had been trained to be off-leash in public if he was behaving. He would simply walk side-by-side with his owners and follow their commands, lucky a dog as he was. He was supposed to stay right next to the kids, or Mom, or Dad, whoever was taking charge of him.

Thank goodness they're finally taking

this leash off, Rosco thought.

Meanwhile, the family was ready for the petting zoo. On every visit, Mandy especially loved to see the chickens. They weren't cute and cuddly, except for the baby chicks, but they were neat. She liked their clawed feet and the funny way they strutted about. She had recently been begging her dad to let the kids get chickens at home.

"We'll see, Mandy. A chicken coop is a lot of work."

The piglets were James's favorite. Every year he tried to pick one up. But they were usually too quick to catch.

Their dad always got in on the action too, no stranger to farm animals. He had grown up on a farm, so he approached the animals easily. He fed them kibble from his hands. He inhaled that farm fresh smell with joy—cow patty stench and all. The kids, on the other hand, wrinkled their noses and squealed. Dad would just laugh.

Mom always stood outside the corral and

took photos. She loved coming to the farm but wasn't such a fan of hopping over the rabbit droppings, or allowing those sharp chicken beaks so close to her legs. Plus, the animals made her sneeze. She always preferred to stay outside the fence and watch.

The kids filed into the petting corral. Mom squinted in front of her camera. Dad fumbled for change to use at the goat food dispenser.

Rosco was proud of himself after his sheep herding work, but he wasn't ready to see that goose again any time soon. So he waited outside the gate and lay down for a nap in the sunshine.

It's nice to rest, Rosco thought, enjoying his nap. He was tired from all of the running around. He listened to the sounds that he now knew were ducks, sheep, pigs, and a goose.

In a short while, however, his ears perked up as a loud engine started. He sat up and saw a parked tractor that would pull a hay wagon. The hay wagon was filling with people. Rosco jumped to his feet.

Mom was snapping photos and didn't notice when Rosco abandoned his resting spot. He ran to greet the people on the noisy hay wagon. Once again his good-natured doggy smile captured the attention of those at the farm.

"Hop on, pooch!" a boy cheered from the hay wagon. *The kids are busy. I might as well,* he thought. So Rosco did.

The tractor rolled into motion. It was taking the people and now Rosco on a hayride. It left the petting zoo area and began the tour around a field of tall, green and yellow plants.

Soon the hay wagon came upon a sign that read: Corn Maze Starts Here. Good luck! The children on the ride begged their parents to let them come back and try the maze later.

The hayride passed several large, rustic, wooden cutouts of friendly ghosts, smiling wicked witches, cuddly farm animals next to a barn, and pretty colorful trees with the leaves falling off. All sorts of charming autumn displays were pictured along the edge of the cornfield.

Rosco stood in front of some friendly boys who were petting his back and wondering out loud where Rosco's owner might be. But a movement at the edge of the cornfield caught Rosco's eye.

A rabbit, was it? It was! The rabbit paused to nibble on some grass.

The rabbit was brown with a cottony white tail. It paid no attention to the hay wagon or Rosco.

I have to leave it alone! I promised my people! This time I'll obey! I won't chase anything! Rosco thought.

The tractor's engine let out a loud puff, alarming the rabbit. The rabbit fled.

Rosco held his position on the wagon, willing every bone in his body to stand still and not chase the rabbit. The rabbit disappeared down a narrow opening in the corn.

Rosco breathed a sigh of relief. *Whew. I did it! Lucky break. Good dog!* He congratulated himself.

The hayride continued on. Now they were passing some people-sized, people-like figures. But these were not people. They were scarecrows.

A scarecrow dressed as a chef stood in front of him. It had a pumpkin for a head. It also had a wide, black, fancy, mustache over

its jack-o-lantern mouth, and a tall white chef's hat on its head.

The hayride kept moving. Another scarecrow dressed as a baseball player with bat and glove was next. A baseball cap sat on its pumpkin head. Rosco extended his gaze down the path. Another, this one a nurse in full white uniform, had a hospital chart in her scarecrow arm. *Well, this is all very interesting.*

Rosco rode along, amazed by the scarecrows. The rabbit was now barely a memory.

Just then, Rosco saw some kids in black T-shirts darting through the corn inside the maze. They were laughing in scary voices and seemed to be chasing some other kids who were screaming. The tractor's engine was very loud so it appeared as though no one else on the hayride had noticed the screaming and chasing. Only Rosco, with his powerful ears, had heard. And he thought it was strange, because the kids being chased didn't sound like they were enjoying themselves. They sounded afraid.

The hayride continued, and soon the kids in the maze were out of view.

They passed a ninja warrior and a scary clown scarecrow that made Rosco growl and let out a nasty bark. Then they came upon a scarecrow boy and girl.

Maybe they were supposed to be Jack and Jill from the nursery rhyme, thought Rosco. They were holding a bucket between them and were dressed in old-fashioned clothes like Rosco had seen in Mandy's fairy tale books.

This reminded him of his own boy and girl who might be worrying about him by now. He jumped straight off the hay wagon, onto the dirt road, and raced back toward the petting zoo.

CHAPTER 6

THE CORN MAZE

Fortunately, the kids and Dad were just leaving the petting zoo and hadn't noticed that Rosco had even left. They were talking about how hungry they were.

"Well it's about eleven o'clock," Mom said. "I guess it's not too early for lunch."

Each person in the family had a sausage sandwich, piled high with onions and cabbage. Even Rosco was given a sausage.

Now it was time for the corn maze. They raced over to the entrance to begin. This was Mandy's favorite part of the day. "This and everything else!" she told her mother.

Admission to the maze always came with

a scavenger hunt entry that looked like a bingo card. The numbers one through nine were in boxes on the page, three across and three down.

Hidden in the corn maze were real mailboxes, and in each mailbox were an inkpad and a stamp. The stamp was in the shape of a Halloween character or an autumn symbol, like a bat or a leaf.

The idea was to find each of the nine mailboxes and stamp your card in the right box, with the character found there, until you had all nine stamps on your bingo card.

For instance, if you spotted a mailbox with the number four on it, you'd look inside the mailbox and find a squirrel stamp. You would take the squirrel stamp, press it into the inkpad, and stamp the number four spot on your bingo card with it.

This had to be done for every number. Once you had stamped all nine boxes, you'd have completed the whole scavenger hunt. And if you completed it, you won a prize at the end!

This year the prize was a treat bag filled with candy corn. Candy corn was one of the kids' favorite things about autumn.

To James and Mandy, this candy corn prize was even better than last year's. And last year's was pretty good. It had been a

voucher for a free piece of grilled corn at the BBQ stand. They had won. That real corn was delicious and tasted like a little piece of summer.

"But candy corn is even more amazing!" Mandy joked. "Get it? A-*maze*-ing?" James groaned. Mom chuckled.

They couldn't wait to begin. But James wanted to do the maze his own way this year.

"Dad, I'm ten years old now. I'm not a little kid anymore. And Rosco is here with us, and he's such a smart dog," he started.

"Can Mandy and I do the maze alone this year without you and Mom, as long as Rosco stays with us? Please! He'll keep us safe. We'll stick together. And we won't fight! I promise! We'll even share a bingo card so we HAVE to stick together. Please?"

James and Mandy always wanted to see who could finish things first, whether it was a running race, a board game, or even a sentence, sometimes. Dad looked squarely at James, then at Mandy.

Well, this is unusual, Dad thought. *I'd love to see them cooperating on something for a change. And sharing a bag of candy without fighting? I haven't seen that happen in a while...*

Dad raised his eyebrows and focused on Rosco. Rosco sat—obedient, serious, and looking ready for the job.

"Well..." Dad looked up at the sunny sky, squinted his eyes, and gazed at the tall rows of corn in the distance. He was trying to see just how far back the field stretched. It was huge, and the hayride that was now in progress and about to turn and follow the dirt road behind the corn looked only about an inch tall from where he was standing. It was *that* far away.

Dad raised his eyebrows. "That maze looks even bigger than last year, guys. You sure you want to go it alone? You could really get lost in there, you know? You've never done this without us along. Sometimes people get lost in there for hours."

James said quickly, "No, Dad! It won't be a problem! Mandy is good at remembering the twists and turns. And I'm too old to have my mom and dad along now. Besides, Rosco can sniff his way out if we get lost. Please, Dad! Please?"

Mandy chimed in. "Yes, Daddy, please! Pretty please?"

Mom and Dad gave each other a look. The four of them had done this maze for *so* many years now. Every year, although the path changed, it was always manageable. There were obstacles and it certainly got confusing at times, but it was nothing the kids couldn't handle.

"Well, okay. We'll let you do it yourselves. We can't treat you like babies forever, can we?" Dad laughed. But he looked just a little bit worried.

The kids cheered. Rosco stood up and started to wag his black tail.

"I'll sit right here on this bale of hay. I'll give you one hour and if there's no sign of you by then, I'm coming in to look for you. But you know where I'll be if you finish early." He looked at his watch.

Mom laid down the law too. "Stick to the scavenger hunt, then turn around and head right back out. Don't get so excited that you get way off the main trail. And no running! Those paths are uneven and I don't want either of you getting hurt. And stay together— all the way to the end!"

"Alright, alright, Mom. We know."

Finally, she bent down to give Rosco his orders. "And you, boy, keep an eye on these two! No monkey business!"

Plenty of older children like the McKendricks were entering the maze. They too, were allowed to explore it on their own. Mrs. McKendrick looked around, scanning the area.

A herd of parents sat and waited on hay bales outside the entrance. The sitting area was covered with a canopy to shade them from the hot sun. Some parents chatted with each other. Others pushed strollers back and forth, keeping babies happy. Dusty maze paths were not an easy place for stroller wheels.

Only a short distance from the entrance a sign over the exit read: You Made It! Exit Maze. A few kids were posing for a photo under the sign.

Mom smiled, sighed and grabbed her camera, gesturing for them to stand at the entrance. She snapped a picture of Mandy, James and Rosco with the sign behind them.

"You kids are growing up too fast!" she exclaimed. She squeezed James at the shoulders and circled Mandy with one arm. "Alright, now have fun in there!"

Mandy grabbed their scavenger hunt card. They were both excited to be out on their own. They skipped off with Rosco on their heels.

Mom watched in hesitation, and then turned to her husband. "Hmm...No sense in both of us waiting here. Why don't I go load up on our favorites at the farm store while you wait here for the kids? That way we might beat traffic on the way home." Dad always loved to beat traffic.

She handed him Rosco's leash. "Do you mind holding this, so I don't have to hold it in the store?"

CHAPTER 7

THE JEWEL OF THE NEIGHBORHOOD

Usually, after the McKendricks had their fill of the farm activities, they'd hit the store together. Here they'd buy dad's favorites—toasted walnuts and salted sunflower seeds. They'd always buy mom's favorite too—sugar coated peanuts.

This was a treat for Mom, to be able to stroll through the fall decorations without the kids begging for every color of taffy at the candy counter or Dad asking her if she was done yet.

The store was always crowded on Saturdays in the fall and only the most patient of shoppers could find peace and enjoyment among the busy crowds of customers. Mom loved it. Dad, on the other hand, usually wanted in and then wanted out.

Mom sniffed one of the candles lining the shelves. It smelled like cinnamon. Right then and there she vowed to bake a homemade apple pie tomorrow. Apple was Mandy's favorite.

Mom browsed and let her thoughts wander. *I'll guess we'll go out to the pumpkin patch when the kids get back...*Usually, when the family was done in the maze, it would be time to take on dad's ultimate challenge—to find the biggest pumpkin that he could possibly lift without hurting his back.

"Our dad is some sort of crazy genius pumpkin carver!" the kids told their friends every October.

He insisted that they visit this particular farm because it grew such enormous pumpkins. Every year he tried to top his previous creation. Most important, size—he liked the whoppers.

The first year he had brought home a pumpkin that weighed eighty pounds. It was almost two feet wide, and Mandy and James then three and six years old, had been able to sit on it side-by-side.

The next year, dad's choice pumpkin had been 101 pounds, and last year, a whopping 120 pounds! These pumpkins were big, and the family's choices were getting bigger every year.

And did they ever make great jack-o-lanterns! Dad researched new spooky designs each year on the Internet before he began to carve, carefully drawing his design onto the pumpkin's best side.

Then he'd set to work making the transformation from pumpkin to jack-o-lantern.

First came cutting out a proper lid. You had to make zigzagged lines around the stem. It made the stem really easy to lift out of the pumpkin, in order to insert the candles.

After the lid was done, Mandy got in on

the action and helped Dad pull out all the goop that stuck to the insides of the gourd. It was stringy and sticky. James called it *just plain yuck*. But Mandy thought it was cool to get her hands so dirty. She was Dad's right-hand girl on that job.

Although the goop was not James's favorite thing about carving a pumpkin, he did love using the cutting tools. Dad let both kids use the tiny but very sharp tools that he bought especially for carving pumpkins. They had metal blades and orange plastic handles. They worked very well.

With the goop came the seeds, and Mom always took those and roasted them, after she cleaned them off. She sprinkled them with salt and then put them in the oven for twenty minutes. The seeds tasted like perfection on a plate.

Dad would snack on them, and then work quietly on his own, grinning and grunting and losing himself in his art. Usually it took about an hour and then the final piece was ready to reveal.

When he was done, the front of the giant pumpkin would have become a horrifying face. It might have pointed eyebrows and an open mouth that seemed to scream "Boo!" at first glance.

Or as in another year, the pumpkin might have been carved into a black cat with a raised tail and long whiskers. Although eerie and quiet, it still seemed to hiss.

No matter what the creation, it would always fill onlookers with wonderful Halloween jitters—the jitters that make kids shriek with delight year after year.

Each year Dad's jack-o-lantern would be

set with four little candles on the inside. The candles would flicker in the dark as the pumpkin sat on the McKendrick family's front porch.

Their giant jack-o-lantern would be the jewel of the neighborhood, every year. Trick-or-treaters would marvel at the size of it. Dad always loved the compliments.

So this day was about more than just petting zoos and hay rides for the McKendrick family. It was about finding another outrageously large pumpkin in that patch. It was about art and tradition.

As the holiday approached, the whole block at home would be anxiously waiting to see what new creation Mr. McKendrick would come up with this year. And trick-or-treaters would come from far and wide to delight in the spectacle on Halloween night!

A text message on her phone interrupted mom's thoughts as she browsed the shop. It was from Dad:

It's been forty-five minutes. Thought they'd be back by now. I'm going in. Meet us at the maze exit in 15 minutes.

CHAPTER 8

STAMPS AND MAILBOXES

Meanwhile, Rosco was enjoying the maze. There were more of the pumpkin-headed scarecrow people inside the maze, too. He was truly impressed.

In their quest to find the first few mailboxes, he and the kids had passed scarecrows that Mandy had called a navy pilot, a rag doll, and a cowboy from the Wild West! The cowboy wore a hat and carried a pistol. Rosco sniffed each one up and down.

"Look, James! There's another mailbox!" Mandy yelped.

James stopped a few steps ahead of his sister. They both peeked between the stalks of corn. Sure enough, there stood another white mailbox. They hurried along the trail and turned a corner. Rosco followed closely, tail wagging with excitement.

It was the black cat stamp, number eight on the card. Mandy stamped it—two more stamps to find.

The mailboxes were not in any particular order inside the maze. The numbers didn't give you any clue about your location because that would make it too easy to find your way out.

By placing the mailboxes out of numerical order, the planners had found a way to make the maze much more confusing and a lot less logical. But that was also what made it so much fun.

For Mandy and James and Rosco, as far as the hunt went, so far, so good. They still had to find the stamps in the shapes of the spider web and the acorn. They had found all seven others. But they were getting tired.

They continued walking and hunting.

Forty-five minutes had passed on James's watch.

"My feet hurt," said Mandy.

"I'm getting really thirsty," said James. The hot sun was blazing down, straight overhead now. "We're supposed to be back in fifteen more minutes or Dad will start to worry. I don't know how we'll find the last two that fast."

Rosco's doggy smile had started to fade to a tired and thirsty pant. *This is a long walk we're going on,* he thought.

They turned another corner but it was a dead end. No mailbox.

"Let's just keep at it. We're almost done." Mandy said. They kept walking.

Just then Rosco noticed a familiar scent. Then he heard a noise—movement within the cornfield. He looked about. There it was, another rabbit, just like the one that had darted inside the cornfield while he rode the hay wagon.

Rosco had by now become a little bored with the maze since the rows of corn all looked the same. He had been obedient for so long now that he didn't have much willpower left to ignore the rabbit. Like any distracted puppy, he pounced.

But he missed. The rabbit moved quickly away, and that old chasing instinct just took over! Rosco forgot his strict orders and his sworn promise. He ran and didn't look back.

Mandy called out but Rosco ignored her. *This will only take a minute. Then I'll be right back. They'll catch up to me in no time,* he thought. *I've got to catch that rabbit!* Off he dashed.

Mandy sighed a long, drawn-out sigh. "Oh Rosco, not again..."

CHAPTER 9

LOST IN
THE STALKS

Mr. McKendrick took a deep breath as he walked through the maze.

I'm sure they're fine. Just keep walking. You'll find them, Dad thought.

He had been searching for ten minutes and there was no sign of his children. *Plenty of other kids around—everyone's having fun. Nothing's wrong.*

But he checked his watch again, trying to ignore the worried feeling. *Oh boy, why did I say they could go alone?*

Meanwhile, the kids were not in any sort of trouble. They were just disappointed in

their dog. He became distracted so easily.

"Why does he just run off like that? Doesn't he think we'll get worried?" James said to no one in particular.

Their dog had run off to chase a rabbit and now, he was nowhere to be found. That old rascal in him had come back just when Rosco was supposed to be on his best behavior.

The kids walked on, hoping for any sign of their dog. Maybe they'd get lucky and find another mailbox on the way.

"Rosco! Rosco!" Mandy called. "Where are you?"

Ignoring his thirsty tongue and his tired legs, James studied the path in front of them as they walked. He liked taking measurements using only his eyes.

The corn stalks were probably ten feet tall, James guessed, as high as the ceilings at school. Cornstalks were all around them now. The kids couldn't see outside the maze anymore except for the blue sky.

We must be in deep, he thought. They had walked a long way.

Dead yellow leaves from the stalks lay on the ground at the sides of the dirt path. It looked like the leaves would dry out, then eventually fall to the bottom of the corn plant.

Every time they stepped on a leaf it crackled and crunched.

Now and then the kids kicked pebbles in the dirt path just to pass the time.

"How far do you think he could have gotten?" Mandy asked, not really expecting an answer. Then she called out again, "Rosco! Roscooooo! Where are you?"

No bark, no rustling in the corn, no jingling of the tags on his collar. She was really beginning to worry.

"What if we can't find him?"

"He won't get lost, Mandy. He's too smart." James tried to assure her. "He's lousy at chasing fast little animals. He'll lose that rabbit in no time and come trotting back down this path. I'm sure of it. He *is* good at tracking us down." *But I sure wish I still had that leash with me when he does.*

Mandy felt a little better. But five more minutes passed and still, there was no sign of Rosco.

CHAPTER 10

NO TIME FOR PLAY

Meanwhile, farther ahead in the corn maze, Rosco pounced once more at the pile of yellow corn leaves in front of him. He thought the rabbit was right in front of him, between the cornstalks where he was standing. But it wasn't. The rabbit was once again long gone.

Rosco stopped to look around. *Oh well, I guess I'd better find the kids now. They'll be worried.*

Just then a sound caught his attention. Rosco froze, listening.

He heard some boys' voices, in whispers and laughter, and the voices sounded familiar. They were the voices he'd heard

57

earlier on the hayride! He heard the dead leaves rustle and one of them say "Shhhh! Put your mask on! Here comes someone!"

Rosco couldn't see what was happening because a row of cornstalks blocked his view.

He heard more rustling, and all of a sudden he heard them holler "Boo!" in a frightening way. "You'd better run, little boy! We're going to get you! Heh heh heh!"

A child screamed in fear. Rosco heard more rustling and then the sound of two running feet, then lots more quick footsteps running in the other direction.

Rosco's eyes grew wide. And his instinct to protect this child grew strong.

Rosco looked one way and then the other trying to figure out the fastest way to get to the child from behind a wall of cornstalks. He turned left and ran.

In just a few seconds, he heard yet another cry. It was the child again, but this time he cried out in pain.

"Owwwwww!" he cried. "Ouch!"

Rosco relied on his tracking instinct and his excellent hearing. German shepherds, with their front-facing pointed ears, can hear four times better than humans, and Rosco made the most of it.

Rosco quickly rounded a bend. He found the boy sitting on the ground. The kids who'd scared him had disappeared.

Trembling at the sight of this great big dog that had appeared out of nowhere, the little boy tightened his shoulders, his eyes growing wide.

Rosco approached gently. *I won't hurt you,* Rosco thought. Whimpering, he tilted his head to one side. This approach worked.

"Doggy?" the boy said softly. "Can you help me?"

The four-year-old boy had fallen and twisted his ankle. He was clutching it in pain. Tears were streaming down his face.

"My leg hurts!"

Rosco sniffed at his brown hair and the baseball cap lying on the ground next to him.

He nudged the boy's shoulder with his wet nose. Then he padded around, examining him from the other side.

"Those mean kids! They scared me! I'm lost." He sniffled. "I can't find my brothers!"

Rosco had not noticed any mailboxes in quite some time. He and the boy were now far from the heavily used paths. *How did this little boy get so far out here, all alone?* He wondered. *And how will I get him out if he can't walk on his own?*

Rosco looked around, trying to decide what to do. He looked at the boy and barked, then turned and ran back down the path. He would go get help. James and Mandy couldn't be too far from here, he knew.

But the boy panicked. "Don't leave me!" he called. "Wait, doggy! Come back! Please!"

Rosco ran back to the boy. He'd have to try something else. *Don't worry, kid. I'll stay.*

He started barking again, this time in his loudest voice, standing right next to the boy. Someone would hear him eventually.

CHAPTER 11

SHORTCUTS

"Listen—I think it's Rosco! I can hear him!" Mandy shouted.

"Me too! He doesn't sound that far away," said James. "Let's go!"

They hurried in the direction of the barking.

"Remember what Mom said about no running," Mandy called.

"I know. I know," said James. "You don't have to remind me!"

The barking was getting closer. It seemed like Rosco would be right around the next bend. But he wasn't. He wasn't around the next either. So they half-walked, half-scampered along as fast as they could, following the noise, careful not to trip on the uneven ground.

Rosco heard them and knew James and Mandy were close.

The child heard the kids' footsteps, too. "Someone's coming," he said to Rosco. "That means someone heard you! I'll be ok. Go find them now, doggy!"

Rosco dashed off down the trail to find his owners.

But the rows of corn were thick and hard to see through. Mandy and James weren't quite sure how many more paths they'd have to follow before they reached Rosco.

"Wait, there he is!" James said, peering through the cornstalks. "I see some black fur and a wagging tail! He's about five rows over."

"How are we going to get there before he runs off again?" Mandy said, biting her lip.

"Good point. He probably won't stay in one place for long. And that way's going to take too long," he said, nodding at the path ahead. "Let's cut through here." He pushed an opening between two cornstalks. "Look— it's a shortcut!"

Soon they came upon their dog.

"Rosco! Oh Rosco!" Mandy cried. "You had us so worried!"

She hugged him and petted his soft black ears. Rosco panted and smiled, thrilled at the reunion.

But quickly, Rosco turned and began to cut back through the cornstalks from where he had come.

"Where's he going, James?" Mandy said, wrinkling her brow.

"I don't know, but let's go see!"

CHAPTER 12

THE QUEEN'S SEAT

The kids pushed through more rows of cornstalks behind Rosco.

"Oh my goodness—it's a little boy!" Mandy exclaimed.

"What happened to you?" said James, addressing the boy. He and Mandy squatted down next to him.

His face was dirty and his tears had dried, but he had a big smile of relief on his face. His scavenger hunt bingo card was lying on the ground next to him, bent and dirty.

"Hi! I fell and my leg hurts. I can't walk!" he said. "Some scary boys jumped out at me so I ran away. Then I tripped and fell."

He said his name was Luke. He had brown hair and wore jeans and sneakers. Placing his baseball cap back on his head, he told them he was four years old.

"But why were you all alone out here?" Mandy asked.

"Well, I was looking for the mailboxes with my big brothers and I thought I knew where one was. But they wouldn't listen to me and go back to look for it," Luke said sharply. "They said I'm too little, so how would I know where to go? So I waited, real quiet, 'til they walked ahead. Then I went back to look for that mailbox by myself."

"Do you think they noticed you were gone?" Mandy asked.

"I don't know. My big sister's with them, too. She's six. And I couldn't walk as fast as all of them. So maybe not."

"Well, I'm sure they must be looking for you by now," James said. "What about your mom and dad?"

"Well, my baby brother who's one doesn't

walk too fast, and my mom was watching him so she said to go ahead without her and she'd meet us outside the maze. And my dad's phone rang from work, so he stopped helping us hunt. He was gonna catch up in a little while."

James and Mandy looked very concerned.

"Don't worry, we'll get you out of here,

Luke," said James.

"And we'll find your mom and dad, too," Mandy said.

"And I hope we find those boys who scared you. I'd like to give them a little taste of their own medicine," James added. "What did they look like?"

Rosco's ears perked in attention.

"They were wearing black shirts and black masks with creepy skeleton faces."

"Wow, I bet that really scared you, buddy," said James. *What creeps,* he thought.

"I think we'd better just try to get Luke out of here," Mandy said. "*If* we see them we can work on that. Anyway, since Luke can't walk all that way on a sore ankle, I think I have a good idea. Why don't we use the Queen's Seat to carry him?"

"Hmm. That *is* a good idea," James agreed.

"I'll help you stand up first, Luke," said Mandy.

Mandy put her right arm under Luke's

left arm, and helped him up. Luke was really little and still looked so upset. The kids felt sorry for him.

Luke waited, standing on one foot, leaning on Rosco so he wouldn't fall over, while Mandy and James got ready to carry him out.

Mandy and James turned and faced one another. They each crossed their arms in an X shape. Then they grabbed hold of each other's hands and bent down to get to Luke's level.

"Now, sit right down here on our arms," James instructed. "See, it's a seat."

Luke sat down carefully.

"Now, put your arms around our necks," James said.

Luke obeyed, shifting into place. "It *is* a seat!"

"See, it's called the Queen's Seat! I guess we should call it a King's Seat for you, though! You'll be the king!" Mandy said.

"Wow, neat!" said Luke.

CHAPTER 13

THE PLAN

It took a long time to get through the maze walking sideways and carrying another child. The kids weren't even sure they were heading in the right direction. There were few, if any landmarks this far out in the maze to help mark the way. The dressed-up scarecrow people had all been near the beginning of the maze. So everything looked the same now, row after row, turn after turn.

Rosco walked a few steps ahead of the kids. Both kids' legs were starting to ache.

Just then Rosco heard rustling in the corn again, from farther ahead. He halted to listen.

"Be quiet, Joe!" one of the voices said. "More people are coming! Hide, before they see us!"

The kids had noticed Rosco's ears perk up but they hadn't heard the voices. They stopped and set Luke down to rest their arms.

"What's up with Rosco?" Mandy asked, looking around.

Just then, they saw a flash of black T-shirts and skeleton masks—two boys dodging through the cornstalks. The boys were about a hundred yards away and had looked to be about James's size.

"It's those boys who scared me!" Luke whispered. Rosco's ears went back and he growled softly.

"And I bet they're going to try and scare us now, too," said Mandy, frowning.

"I have an idea," James said quietly. "I don't think they know we saw them. Let's keep walking. Then when they jump out at us, let's teach them a lesson." Mandy and Luke agreed to the plan.

So the kids put Luke back on their arms and continued walking as if they had seen nothing. Rosco fell in quietly behind them, guarding from the rear. In another minute, they reached the spot where the boys were hiding.

Sure enough, the masked boys jumped out and shrieked at the kids in frightening low voices. "Boo! Heh Heh Heh! You'd better run! We're going to get you!" They ran toward the kids, waving their arms, then circled around for a second time. Taunting and laughing, their ghoulish skeleton masks were more frightening than the kids had expected. "You're in big trouble! You'd better run!"

Startled and spooked by the ambush, despite their plan, Mandy and James had nearly lost their balance in the commotion. They set Luke down quickly so they wouldn't drop him.

"James?" Mandy whispered, a little frightened. "What do we do now?"

Nostrils flaring and chin held high,

James stood strong but tongue-tied. He'd been surprised at the cruelty in the boys' voices and wasn't sure how to proceed. "I, I..." He choked.

Just then Rosco came from behind the kids, growling and baring his big, sharp, teeth. He hadn't been spooked by the boys' threats.

"Ruff! Ruff! Ruff, ruff, ruff!" He barked viciously.

The boys froze. Their laughter stopped,

and they ripped off their skeleton masks to get a better look at the dog. They both stepped back quickly.

"Call off your dog!" the first one shouted.

"Not, not until you say you're sorry to this little boy," James said, regaining his senses. Rosco stopped barking and stood guard, letting James take over.

"How's it feel to be scared?" James continued. "You scared this boy really badly earlier, and then he sprained his ankle running from you. A little kid—he was all alone and you scared him!"

James went on. "He could've been out here all day, maybe even into the night, if that dog hadn't come along. You'd better thank our dog that nothing worse happened to him, because it would've been *your* fault."

Rosco snarled as James spoke. He barked again.

"Well, we didn't mean for anyone to get hurt," the second one said.

Mandy spoke up, bolder now that James

had started. "You might not have *meant* to, but that's what happened. And you didn't even bother to check to see if he was okay! What do you think a little kid like that was doing out here all by himself? He was obviously L-O-S-T."

She spelled out the word to make her point. "Why would you pick on a lost little kid and think that's okay? You should've seen that he needed help, and then you should've done something about it!" She was really getting fired up. "Instead, you just saw an easy target, and then you scared him out of his wits!"

"Well, so what? We were just having fun," the first boy said rudely. But he was watching Rosco out of the corner of his eye and looking worried. He elbowed his friend in the ribs so that he would say something. But his friend was still frozen in fear, staring at Rosco's sharp teeth, which were only a few feet away from his pant leg.

"N-n-n-nice dog. Please don't hurt me,"

the friend begged.

"What do you mean, you were just having fun?" said Mandy. "Scaring a bunch of kids from behind a mask is your idea of fun? Not even showing your faces? That's what cowards do. That's not how to have fun."

"Okay, okay! I'm sorry!" the first one said. "Now, can you call off your dog?"

The second one mumbled an apology. Neither could take his eyes off of Rosco.

James looked at Rosco, and then at the boys. "Not until you promise that you'll stop scaring kids in the maze. Just get out of here and stop ruining people's fun."

"Aw, come on! You can't tell us what to do," the first one said boldly.

"Maybe not, but *he* can!" James pointed to Rosco. Rosco growled and started barking at them again, inching closer to the boys.

"Okay, okay! We'll stop! No more scaring in the maze!" they yelled. "Can you make him stop now?"

"We'd better not hear about you breaking

your promise, because this dog can sniff out and find anyone," said James coolly.

James waited until Rosco had settled down a bit. "Alright Rosco, you can leave 'em alone now."

"Come on, Nick, let's go!" the first one said to his friend. The boys quickly began to walk away, holding their masks in their hands. They glanced back several times to make sure the dog wasn't following them.

"Good boy, Rosco." James patted his dog's head.

Mandy shouted to the boys. "And by the way, Halloween's still a whole month away if you hadn't noticed!"

James turned to Rosco. "Wow, Rosco, you sure saved me there! Good boy! Thanks!" he said, petting Rosco on the head. Rosco panted. *No problem, James.*

Luke, who had been quietly watching, now sniffled and smiled. The ordeal had frightened him all over again.

James knelt down on one knee and

motioned for Luke to climb on his back. "You're not that heavy, Luke. Come on. I'll carry you by myself for a while. Jump on."

CHAPTER 14

YOU MADE IT!

The three kids and Rosco continued on their way out of the maze. Luke felt a lot better, having watched his new friends stand up for him. James and Mandy felt a lot better for having taken a stand.

Everyone was pleased with the way things had turned out, including Rosco.

"This here dog is like having our own personal army!" Mandy joked. She skipped ahead, still watching for rocks and holes in the path.

Eventually the conversation turned to what was left of their scavenger hunt. James and Mandy still had two more mailboxes left to find—two more stamps left to fill the card. Luke had five left.

But they knew there was no way they could go looking for mailboxes now. They needed to get straight to the exit, just as soon as they could find it.

And once they got out of the maze and found Luke's family, it would take too long to go back into the maze. And their own parents would be worried sick by then, too. But they'd never win the prize if they didn't finish the whole scavenger hunt card.

"It doesn't matter, Mandy," James said. "It's just some candy corn anyway. Not that big of a deal. We can always do it next year." James was trying to convince himself as well as his sister that giving up on the game would be fine. He shifted Luke higher on his back. The boy had begun to slide down a little.

"You're right..." Mandy sighed.

She felt bad that they wouldn't win the prize. But she didn't want Luke to know because he'd feel like it was his fault.

She looked at his face. He looked sad, she thought, just a scared little boy. And she realized she had only been thinking about herself. Helping someone was more important than winning a prize.

"Yeah, you're right, James," she repeated, this time with a little more enthusiasm. "Let's forget about the hunt. No big deal."

Luke said, "Thanks for taking care of me. Sorry to ruin your scavenger hunt."

"It's okay, Luke. Don't worry about it. Really. We're sorry you won't get any candy corn either," said Mandy.

They stopped to take a break. Luke carefully hopped down, and stood on one foot. Then Luke held onto James's waist so he didn't fall. They all stretched their tired muscles.

"You guys are really nice," Luke said.

Just then Rosco ran ahead. He thought he might be picking up the scent of a familiar cowboy scarecrow.

"What is it, Rosco?" called James. "Wait

up!"

In another part of the maze, Dad was still wandering about. He had seen a lot of kids on the hunt, but none of them were his. He was really starting to worry now. It had been a total of an hour and ten minutes since he had said goodbye to the kids at the maze entrance.

They've got to be finishing up by now, he thought. *Maybe it really took them the whole hour. Maybe they're actually done and out by the exit, just waiting for me.*

But I'm not there! He panicked. *Oh no! But of course, Mom should be by now.* He thought, calming himself down again. He turned around and headed back toward the front of the maze.

Meanwhile, Rosco and his gang of three were finally nearing the front. Rosco skipped a little further ahead to scope out the way. He sniffed out the cowboy scarecrow they'd seen at the beginning of the scavenger hunt and began to bark. The kids followed the sound of his bark.

Soon they found the pilot scarecrow, too, the one Rosco had inspected with such interest when they'd first started. He sniffed this way and that, tracking like a dog on a mission.

They soon passed several mailboxes with numbers they'd already stamped and began to recognize various turns in the path. They were now in an area where lots of other kids were walking the paths.

James was still carrying Luke. He had taken several breaks to rest his arms, but it was becoming a difficult job. Mandy plodded on. They turned a corner and stepped onto another path.

"Just a little further, I think," James huffed. "This looks like one of the paths where we started."

Then, out of nowhere they heard a voice.

"Kids!" Dad shouted. "Kids, wait up! It's me! I've been looking everywhere for you guys!"

They turned around to look.

"Daddy? It's Daddy!" Mandy cried.

James set Luke down.

Mr. McKendrick couldn't believe it either. He had turned a corner, heading for the exit, and wound up only a few yards behind his children!

"Well, hello there!" he said, catching up to them. They explained who Luke was and what had happened to his ankle as Mr. McKendrick put an arm around James's shoulder. Mandy hugged her father.

"Rosco found him, Dad! He ran off to chase a rabbit and the next thing we knew, he found Luke!"

They explained the encounter with the boys in the masks.

"Well now I know why you guys didn't show up when I thought you would!" Dad said, and patted Rosco's head. "Good boy, Rosco! I guess we won't be needing this!" He held up the leash. "Gosh, I thought I'd never find you!"

Mr. McKendrick examined Luke's ankle, making sure it wasn't broken. He picked up Luke and rested him on his waist.

"Now let's go find your mother and father. And *your* mother too, kids! She should be waiting for us by now! This way!"

The kids followed their dad. In another five minutes, a large wooden sign appeared over some posts. In big, black letters, it read: You Made It, Exit Maze.

CHAPTER 15

GOOD DOGGY

Mom was indeed waiting outside the exit for them. She was startled to see her husband carrying a strange child but happy that everyone was okay.

They told Mom the whole story as they walked to the shaded area at the maze entrance. When they got there, a young woman jumped up from a hay bale bench, handed her toddler to one of the older brothers, and ran for Luke. It was Luke's mom.

Mr. McKendrick lowered Luke down and gently handed him to her. "Watch that ankle." He explained the injury.

"Mommy! Mommy!" he bellowed.

"Oh, honey! Where have you been? I've been worried sick!" She took her son, kissed and hugged him, joyful to have him back. Luke started to cry again. He was a little choked up but relieved to see his mother. James and Mandy told her the story once she'd carried him over to where the rest of Luke's family was sitting. She sat her son down on a bale of hay.

Luke's mom said that she'd told the

attendants her four-year-old was missing. They had put out that message over the loudspeaker a couple of times. But the only speakers were right at the front of the maze, so Rosco and the kids hadn't heard it.

"They said they would send out a search party if he didn't show up within the hour," said Luke's mom. "I had to wait out here with my little ones and I wouldn't let my older sons go back in. They could've gotten lost, too."

Luke's mother dialed her husband's cell phone number to let him know that everything was all right. He had been hunting for Luke inside the maze ever since his other kids had found him and explained what happened.

"I'm sorry I ran away from you guys," Luke said, choking back tears.

"We're sorry we didn't listen to you about the mailbox. I bet you were right," said one of his older brothers.

"And we should've kept a closer eye on

you," the other one added.

Their mother raised her eyebrows and nodded her head at her older sons.

"Now we all know better," she said. "Next time, stay together, kids." Then, looking straight at Luke, she added, "And don't go wandering off alone, sweetie!"

She bent over and circled his little head in her arms. "Everything's going to be okay now, honey. I promise. We'll get you to the doctor and he'll fix that ankle up in no time."

Rosco had squeezed in next to Luke, listening and panting. Luke petted Rosco softly on the head. "Rosco's a good doggy," he said, calming.

Then Luke's mom turned to Mandy and James, "I want to thank you kids and your dog from the bottom of my heart. You really saved the day."

CHAPTER 16

A PERFECT GIANT PUMPKIN

It was finally time to visit the actual pumpkin field and pick out Dad's whopper of a pumpkin. The McKendricks headed for the patch.

Dad borrowed a wheelbarrow from the edge of the field where a row of them had been placed for customers.

Quickly the family spread out. The sky was blue and the air was still warm. The fresh smell of vines and leaves filled the air.

The large pumpkins grew on a gentle, green hill. At the top of the hill was a boulder jutting from the ground. It looked like a small stage to Mandy. She ran straight to it, followed by Rosco, and climbed on. Mom followed them and switched her phone to the camera setting.

"Ta-da!" Mandy held out her arms as if she had just finished a dance performance. Rosco barked in approval. "Snap!" went Mom's camera. Mandy took a bow.

"What sort of pumpkin do we want this year, Dad?" James called from several yards away. There were wide, fat ones, and tall, skinny ones. There were odd-shaped ones and perfectly formed ones. Any kind could make really neat jack-o-lanterns.

"Whatever looks good, son!" Dad called.

"Let me help!" Mandy jumped off her stage and joined her father in the search, with Rosco close behind.

Dad rolled each one he liked so that he could see its underside. "You have to check for rot," he said. "Looks can be deceiving from the top." Mandy nodded, turning a smaller pumpkin on its side.

When Dad liked a pumpkin that he

found, and it looked fine underneath, he'd roll it a little more, looking for the best side to carve. He usually didn't know what sort of creation he'd carve when he first picked out his pumpkin, but he needed to be sure there was plenty of good carving surface.

"Come here, guys!" James called. He thought he'd found a winner way out in the middle of the field. Rosco and Mandy bounded across the field as Mom and Dad followed.

"We usually get a big, round one," James said. "This year, let's get a tall, skinny one like this."

"Hmmm. Nice and tall, fairly symmetrical," Dad said, examining it. "Uniform in color, no green left on the fruit. Definitely a good size."

He checked the bottom. "And no rot. Looks like we're in business!"

"Maybe you could carve huge, creepy eyes and a scary nose?" Mandy said. "Maybe some fangs on the mouth..."

At the checkout stand the attendant weighed the pumpkin. It turned out to be 125 pounds. Dad was excited. "Bigger than last year's!"

They had found their whopper. In a few weeks, they'd all make sure it became something spectacular for the holiday.

On the drive home, the kids discussed their loot. They had filled their trunk with this year's giant pumpkin and four average-sized pumpkins for the rest of the family to carve. Mom said that was plenty to decorate the porch at home.

James said he'd carve Rosco's. Mandy said she would clean out the goop for him. Rosco grinned at the thought of finally having his very own pumpkin.

Then Mom pulled out a small bag from the farm store. She hadn't mentioned it earlier when they told her with disappointment how they hadn't finished the scavenger hunt.

"I have a little prize of my own to award the two of you now. For bravery and thoughtfulness, I give you..." She handed the bag to them in the backseat.

"Taffy!" said the kids. "Candy corn flavored taffy? Awesome, Mom! Thanks!"

"And for Rosco, our loveable rascal who has forever changed our visits to the pumpkin patch..." She pulled out another bag. It was a dog biscuit in the shape of a pumpkin. "A pumpkin you can really sink your teeth into!"

Finally! thought Rosco, and he crunched it and ate it all in one bite!

About The Author

Shana Gorian, originally from western Pennsylvania, lives in Southern California with her husband and two children, and the real *Rosco*, their German shepherd. Shana and her family visit the pumpkin patch every fall in search of the perfect giant pumpkin.

Ros Webb is an artist based in Ireland. She has produced a multitude of work for books, digital books and websites. Samples of her art can be seen on Facebook: Ros Webb Book Illustration.

Josh Addessi is a quirky illustrator and animation professor based in Northwest Indiana. He has digitally painted all manner of book covers, stage backdrops and trading cards. Samples of his art can be seen at
http://joshaddessi.blogspot.com/

The *real* Rosco is every bit as loveable, heroic and rascally as the fictional Rosco. He loves to play keep-away, too.

Visit **shanagorian.com** to keep up with Rosco and his upcoming adventures. And be sure to join him for more adventures in the other books in the series!

Made in the USA
Las Vegas, NV
04 October 2023

78572181R00062